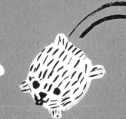

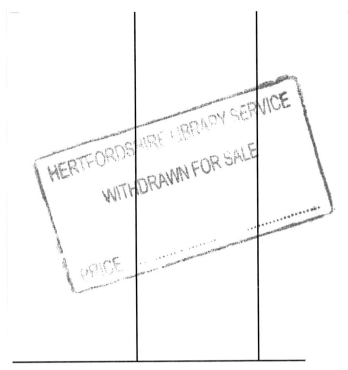

Please renew or return items by th
shown on your receipt

www.hertfordshire.gov.uk/libr₁₄9

Renewals and enquiries: 0300 4041

Textphone for hearing or 0300
speech impaired users:

L32 11.16

528 123 48 8

lemmings: small, fuzzy, illiterate rodents who share the icy North with arctic foxes and polar bears. People used to think lemmings jumped off cliffs. Now we know they don't.

READ THE BOOK, LEMMINGS!

Written by Ame Dyckman

Illustrated by Zachariah OHora

Andersen Press

Foxy found a quiet spot
to read his book
about lemmings.
"Huh!" Foxy said.
"Says here,
lemmings *don't* jump off cliffs."

JUMP?
I'LL JUMP!

said a
lemming.

ME TOO!

said a
second.

DITTO!

said a
third.

"Huh!" said Captain PB.
"Guess they didn't read the book."
Foxy looked.

Foxy sighed. "Sir?" he asked. "May I borrow your bucket?"
"Fine," said Captain PB. "But your lemmings better not eat my fish."

Foxy pulled.

Foxy dumped.

Foxy gave his lemmings names — and hats — so he could scold them properly.

"Focus, Jumper!" Foxy said. "You too, Me Too! Ditto... Ditto."

Foxy opened his book.

"Huh!" said the lemmings.
"Exactly!" Foxy said.
"The book says you *don't.*"
"Don't?" asked Jumper.
"Don't what?"
"Jump off cliffs,"
  Foxy said.

 said
Jumper.

 said
Me Too.

 said
Ditto.

GERONIMO

Foxy groaned. "I hate to ask again…"
"Oh, take it!" grumbled Captain PB.
"My fish already taste like lemmings!"

WHAT WERE YOU THINKING?

Foxy yelled.
"The book says you *don't* j—"
Foxy stopped.
"Just read the book,
lemmings."

AHHHHHHHHH!

said the lemmings.

They took a look and
returned the book.

GERONIMO-O
"Nope!" said Captain PB.
"They definitely didn't
read the book!"

There was no time to use the bucket.
"Watch my book," Foxy said.

Foxy scooped.

Foxy swam.

Foxy flopped.

Foxy blinked.

"Question…"
Foxy asked.

WHY DIDN'T YOU READ THE BOOK, LEMMINGS?!

"Huh!" said Captain PB.
"That's a good start!"

"I'll teach you to read, lemmings,"
Foxy promised.

They practised reading all afternoon.

WE ARE
LEMMINGS!
C IS FOR
CLIFF

Until...

Foxy finally returned to his reading.
But Captain PB could not.

Where's my paper?

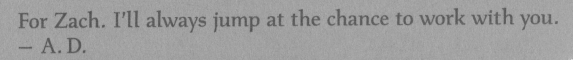

For Zach. I'll always jump at the chance to work with you.
— A. D.

For Ame. This is just the tip of the iceberg.
— Z. O.

Author's Note:

When I was little, I saw a movie that showed lemmings jumping off cliffs. Years later, I learned that, except in very rare cases, lemmings DON'T jump off cliffs. My first thought was, "OH NO! DID ANYONE TELL THE LEMMINGS?!"
So, we made this book. You're welcome, lemmings.

First published in Great Britain in 2018 by Andersen Press Ltd.,
20 Vauxhall Bridge Road, London SW1V 2SA.
Originally published by Little, Brown and Company, Hachette Book Group,
1290 Avenue of the Americas New York, NY 10104, USA
Text copyright © 2017 by Ame Dyckman
Illustrations copyright © 2017 by Zachariah OHora
The rights of Ame Dyckman and Zachariah OHora to be identified as author
and illustrator of this work have been asserted by them in accordance with
the Copyright, Designs and Patents Act, 1988.
All rights reserved.
Printed and bound in China.
10 9 8 7 6 5 4 3 2 1
British Library Cataloguing in Publication Data available.
ISBN 978 1 78344 634 6 (hardback)
ISBN 978 1 78344 655 1 (paperback)